Mabel and Me
Best of Friends

HarperCollins *Children's Books*

First published in hardback in Great Britain by HarperCollins Children's Books in 2013
First published in paperback in 2013
This edition published in 2015

1 3 5 7 9 10 8 6 4 2

ISBN: 978-0-00-758593-9

HarperCollins Children's Books is a division of HarperCollins Publishers Ltd.

Text copyright © Mark Sperring 2013, 2015
Illustrations copyright © Sarah Warburton 2013

Visit our website at: www.harpercollins.co.uk

Printed in China

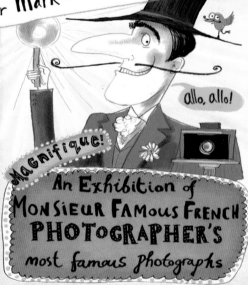

Mabel and Me
Best of Friends

Mark Sperring and Sarah Warburton

One day Mabel and Me are taking a stroll down a strolly street,
when I say, "You know, Mabel, you really are
my bestest,
bestest friend!"

mabel

me

But then Mabel asks a hugely harrowing
and diabolically difficult question. Mabel asks...

I cannot think of a single reason why Mabel
should be my bestest, bestest friend, but luckily,
just then, we are interrupted, and
somebody says...

"Allo, allo, my charming friends! I am a Famous French Photographer. May I take a picture of you and your strange little creature thing?"

I look at Mabel and feel my
nose start to
TWITCH
AND
TREMBLE.
Then I say...

"Hey, Monsieur Famous French Photographer, mind your mannerisms!

How dare you refer to Mabel as a 'strange little creature thing'... Can't you see she's just as tall as me (and only slightly strange)?"

Then I grab hold of Mabel's hand.

"Come on, Mabel," I say,
"let's go and have our picture taken by
a Famous French Photo Booth instead!"

But, just as we sit on the seat and before the Famous French
Photo Booth has even had a chance to go...

FLASH!

click

FLASH!

click

chugga, chugga,

CHUGGA

.............."Voilà! Your pictures!"

Somebody says...

"Look at those perfect pointy toes!"

And, SURPRISE, SURPRISE, it's Señora Prima Ballerina!
She says...

"My dear, I can tell just by looking at you,
you'll make the most extraordinary dancer.
You must join my ballet class, mucho pronto!
Then we can dance on tiptoe all day long."

Mabel and Me nod and smile and raise our
arms in a perfectly graceful arc.
But Señora Prima Ballerina shakes her head.

"No, I didn't mean both of you..."
she says. "Besides, your friend has
such scrawny, hairy rodent legs—
not dancer's legs at all!"

Well,
I cannot believe my furry ears and for at least a moment,
I am TOTALLY lost for words.

In fact,
I am SO
VERY angry
that I cannot even address
Señora Prima Ballerina
in a polite manner.

So I count to ten.

Then, when I have suitably composed myself,

I say...

"Hey, you, you in the tutu!

I would very much prefer it if you did not refer to Mabel's legs as scrawny, hairy rodent legs

(although it's true, they are slightly hairy).

For that reason alone, I cannot accept your 'mucho pronto, dance-all-day-long-on-tiptoe ballet class' offer. Besides, don't you know Mabel and Me only ever dance TOGETHER. We are particularly fond of boom box street dancing, but are also partial to tap and jazz.

So, alas, we must bid you farewell!!

Au revoir! And see you later, alligator!"

Then Mabel and Me dance down the strolly streets

in a

Boom
box,
TAP,

tappity tap)) tap tap tappity)) tap

and **Jazz** kind of way,

while passersby WHOOP and CHEER
and throw off their hats in utter delight.

But the very first moment we get around the corner, I take Mabel by the hand and tell her I'm SO SORRY that she had to hear all those terrible things about herself.

I say
that Monsieur Famous
French Photographer and
Señora Prima Ballerina are
just plain mean
and if I were her, I would
forget all about
them.

But Mabel says I've got it all wrong.
Mabel says that their AWFUL comments were aimed at...

...me!

Well...

I take a deep breath
and feel my fur start to BRISTLE.

"Mabel," I say, "are you SERIOUSLY SUGGESTING that people think of me as a **strange** little creature thing with **scrawny, hairy rodent legs?**"

And, can you BELIEVE it?

Mabel says...

But then, finally and thankfully, I remember one of the
reasons why Mabel is my BESTEST, BESTEST friend.

And I say...
"Oh, Mabel, you are my BESTEST, BESTEST friend because...
you always say the CRAZIEST things!"

Then Mabel and Me laugh long and hard...

...the way that **best friends** always do.

the End